Using 3-D Shapes to
Build Houses

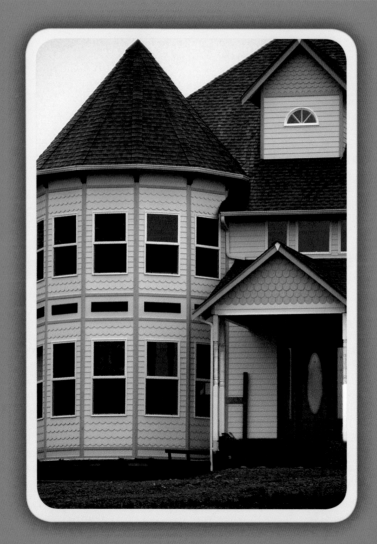

Moira Anderson

Real World Math Books are published by Capstone Press,
151 Good Counsel Drive, P.O. Box 669, Mankato, Minnesota 56002.
www.capstonepub.com

032010
005740CGF10

Library of Congress Cataloging-in-Publication Data
Anderson, Moira (Moira Wilshin)
  Using 3-D shapes to build houses / by Moira Anderson.—1st hardcover ed.
      p. cm. —(Real world math level 4)
  Includes index.
  ISBN 978-1-4296-5241-4 (library binding)
  1. House construction—Juvenile literature. 2. Geometry—Juvenile literature.
  I. Title. II. Series.
  TH4811.5.A625 2011
  690'.8—dc22   2010001820

Editorial Credits
Sara Johnson, editor; Emily R. Smith, M.A.Ed., editorial director; Sharon Coan, M.S.Ed., editor-in-chief;
Lee Aucoin, creative director; Rachelle Cracchiolo, M.S.Ed., publisher

Photo Credits
The authors and publisher would like to gratefully credit or acknowledge the following for permission
to reproduce copyright material: cover Photolibrary.com/Nick Higham; p.1 Big Stock Photo; p.4 (inset)
Photolibrary.com; p. 4 (background) Big Stock Photo; p.5 Big Stock Photo; p.6 Big Stock Photo; p. 7 (top)
Photolibrary.com; p. 7 (bottom) Getty Images/Jochen Luebke; p.9 Big Stock Photo; p.10 Photolibrary.
com/Thomas A. Heinz; p.11 (top) Photolibrary.com/Nick Higham; p.11 (bottom) Getty Images/Alfred
Eisenstaedt; p.12 Big Stock Photo; p.13 Photolibrary.com/Robert W. Ginn; p.14 Photolibrary.com/Bill
Heinsohn; p.15 Photolibrary.com/Dennis Hallinan; p.16 Big Stock Photo; p.17 Big Stock Photo; p.18
Big Stock Photo; p.19 Photos.com; p.20 Big Stock Photo; p.21 (top) Big Stock Photo; p.21 (bottom) Getty
Images/Jeff Smith; p.22 (top) 123 Royalty Free Images; 22 (bottom) Big Stock Photo; p.23 (left) Big Stock
Photo; p.23 (right) Photodisc; p.24 123 Royalty Free Images; p.25 (top) Photolibrary.com/Leonora Gim;
p.25 (bottom) Photos.com; p.26 Photolibrary.com/Esta Hiltula; p.27 (top) Juan Silva; p.27 (bottom)
Photolibrary.com; p.28 Pearson Education Australia/Alice McBroom Photography; p.29 Getty Images.

While every care has been taken to trace and acknowledge copyright, the publishers tender their
apologies for any accidental infringement where copyright has proved untraceable. They would be
pleased to come to a suitable arrangement with the rightful owner in each case.

Table of Contents

Building a Home

Wade's family is going to build a new house on a **plot** of land. The neighborhood is a great place for Wade's family to live. Wade's parents work close by. And his friends live in the area, too.

Wade wonders what their new house will look like. He begins to look at all kinds of homes. He sees many different shapes in the houses.

LET'S EXPLORE MATH

Some houses are made of bricks. A brick is a **three-dimensional (3-D)** shape. It is a rectangular prism. Faces are the flat parts of a 3-D shape. Edges are where 2 faces meet. Look at this rectangular prism.

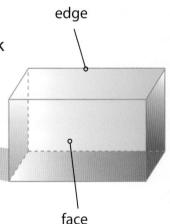

edge

face

a. How many faces does it have?

b. How many edges does it have?

c. Name another 3-D shape that has the same number of faces and edges.

Geometry Around Us

Look at the apartments or houses in your neighborhood. You will see many shapes. The study of shapes is called **geometry**. Geometry is all around us.

What shapes do you see in this picture?

Architects

Architects (AR-kuh-tekts) design buildings. Wade's family meets with an architect. They talk about what their house will look like. Then the architect shows Wade's family a picture of his favorite building. It is a fire station.

Vitra Fire Station, Germany

Zaha Hadid, 1950–

Zaha Hadid is a famous architect. She was born in Baghdad, Iraq. She designed the fire station in the picture above. Zaha has a degree in mathematics.

Shapes for Houses

Architects choose the shapes that make up a building and its rooms. Think about your house or apartment. It is made of many three-dimensional shapes. Rectangular prisms and cubes are good 3-D shapes for rooms.

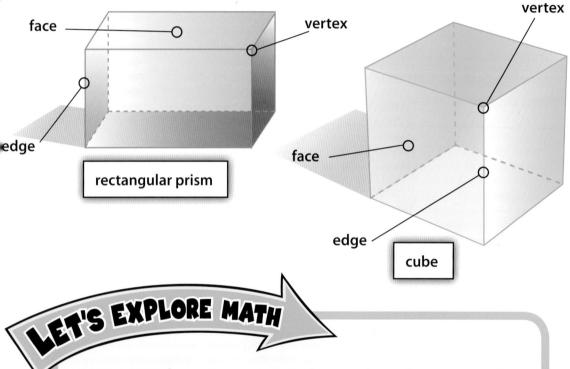

face

vertex

vertex

edge

rectangular prism

face

edge

cube

LET'S EXPLORE MATH

A **vertex** is the point on a 3-D shape where 2 or more edges meet. If you are talking about more than 1 vertex, you say **vertices** (VER-tuh-seez). Use the shapes above to answer these questions.

a. How many vertices does a rectangular prism have?

b. Does a cube have the same number of vertices as a rectangular prism?

House Plans

The family's architect talks about where the rooms should be built. Bedrooms are for sleeping. They should be away from noisy rooms, such as the kitchen.

Next, the architect draws a plan. The plan shows what the house will look like when it is built.

> Architect plans are amazing **two-dimensional** (**2-D**) drawings. Builders follow these plans to make 3-D buildings. Look at this house plan. What 2-D shapes can you see? What 3-D shapes will they be when the house is built?

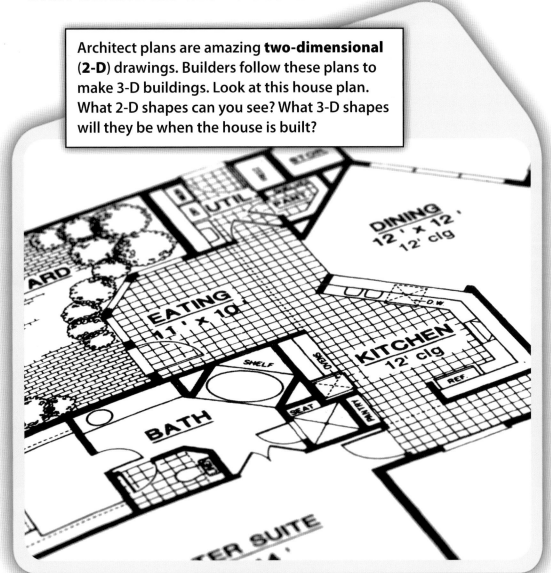

The architect shows Wade and his family some pictures of amazing houses. Wade's family looks closely at the photos to get ideas. Wade notices that the wooden beams and brick columns in this house are shaped like rectangular prisms.

House in Buffalo, New York

Wade sees that each roof for this house looks like a flat rectangular prism. He also reads that this famous house is called "Fallingwater."

Frank Lloyd Wright, 1867–1959

Frank Lloyd Wright is the famous architect who designed these houses. He also designed many museums and office buildings.

The Foundation

It's time for Wade's house to be built. The house is built on a **foundation** called a slab. The slab is made of concrete. It looks like many rectangular prisms joined together.

The concrete slab makes the house **stable**. It will not move if the soil becomes very wet or very dry.

The Floors

The builders lay the wooden frame for the floor on top of the foundation. They cover the frame with more wood to make the floor. Like the concrete slab, the wooden boards for the frame are three-dimensional **solid figures**.

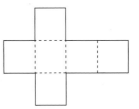

This is a net of a cube. A net is a flat pattern that can be folded to make a 3-D model. Draw a different layout that would make a cube when folded.

Wade begins to dream about his new house. He remembers a visit to a famous house called Hearst Castle. He laughs when he wakes up. He knows their house will not be that fancy!

Julia Morgan, 1872–1957

Julia Morgan designed this house. It is called Hearst Castle. She also designed more than 700 other buildings.

Hearst Castle is in California. It has a large outdoor swimming pool. There are many columns in the buildings near the pool. The columns are shaped like cylinders.

cylinder

The Walls

Next, the builders make wooden frames for the walls. They put the frames up on top of the floors. Now it is easy to see where the rooms will be.

The wooden frames of a house

The Roof

Triangle-shaped wooden frames make the roof. These frames are called **trusses**. The trusses are joined by **timber**. The roof looks like a triangular prism.

Many houses have roofs shaped like triangular prisms. Prisms are named after the shapes of their **bases**. Bases are special faces of solid figures. Usually, prisms sit on one of their bases.

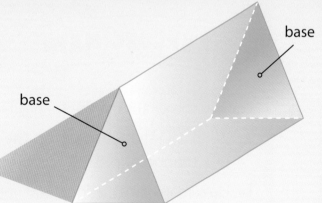

base

base

The trusses are done. Now the builders cover the roof with sheets of wood. These sheets make the roof firm and strong. It will not bend.

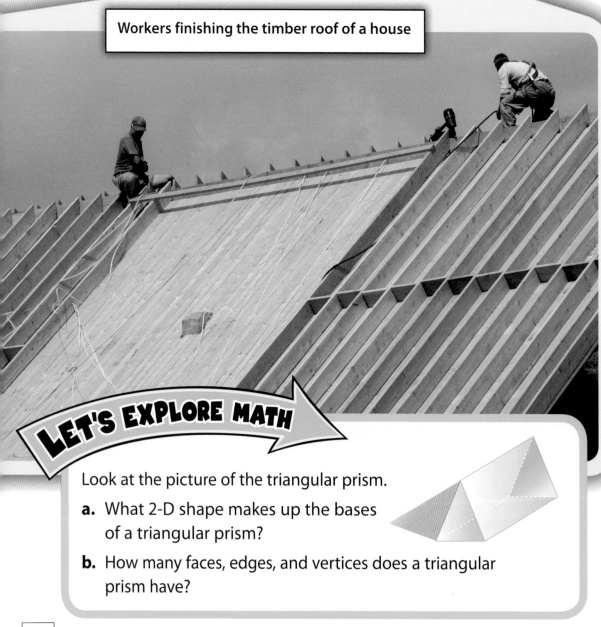

Workers finishing the timber roof of a house

LET'S EXPLORE MATH

Look at the picture of the triangular prism.

a. What 2-D shape makes up the bases of a triangular prism?

b. How many faces, edges, and vertices does a triangular prism have?

Trusses are also used when building bridges. This is because trusses are very strong. Wade remembers seeing steel trusses on a very famous bridge.

The Brooklyn Bridge, New York City

Emily Roebling, 1843–1903

Emily Roebling's (ROH-blings) husband began building the Brooklyn Bridge. Then he became very sick. So Mrs. Roebling took over. The Brooklyn Bridge has steel trusses.

Doors and Windows

Next, the builders put in the doors and windows. Look at the windows. They are rectangles. Rectangles are 2-D shapes. So are the doorways. The doors themselves are tall, skinny rectangular prisms. They are 3-D shapes.

 **LET'S EXPLORE MATH**

Prisms get their names from the shapes of their bases. What are the names of these prisms?

a.   **b.**

Wade notices that another new house is being built in the neighborhood. Its side is shaped a little like a **pentagon**.

I.M. Pei, 1917–

I.M. Pei (PAY) is a famous architect. He designed the glass pyramid for the Louvre (LOO-vrah) Museum in France. He also designed this office building in Hong Kong.

Plumbing and Wiring

Houses need **plumbing** and **wiring**. Plumbers **install** and check the plumbing in the bathrooms and kitchen. Electricians install and check the wiring.

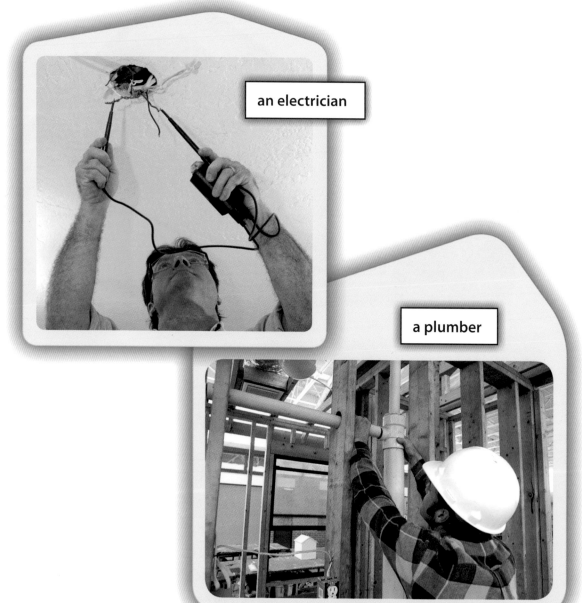

an electrician

a plumber

Think about kitchen or bathroom pipes. What shape are they? They are cylinders. And what shape are electrical wires? They are cylinders, too. There really are 3-D shapes everywhere in houses!

LET'S EXPLORE MATH

There are many cylinders in homes in the pipes and wiring. Look at the diagram of the cylinder above.

a. How many bases and edges does it have?

b. What shape are the bases?

c. How is a cylinder different from a prism?

Inside the House

Next, the builders put up the inside walls. The walls are painted. Counters and cupboards are installed. These are often rectangular prisms.

rectangular prism

Drawers are very useful 3-D shapes.

Wade's mom says there will be plenty of closets in the new house. This will give Wade places to store his things.

Jørn Utzon, 1918–2008

Some people think of Jørn Utzon's (yorn OOT-zuhns) architecture as art. He designed the famous Sydney Opera House in Sydney, Australia. The building is near the bay. Its roof is shaped like waves.

How many boxes shaped like rectangular prisms can you see?

Living in 3-D

Lastly, the outside of the house is painted. A water **feature** is put in the garden. It looks like a huge sphere!

sphere

LET'S EXPLORE MATH

Look at the diagram of the sphere above.

a. How many edges and vertices does it have?

b. It is very unusual to use spheres when building a home. Why do you think this is?

Now, the house is finished. The new house is strong and solid. It is time for Wade and his family to move in and unpack!

Frank Gehry, 1929–

Frank Gehry (GAIR-ee) uses unusual shapes in his designs. Some people say this museum looks like a ship. Others say the outside looks like a fish.

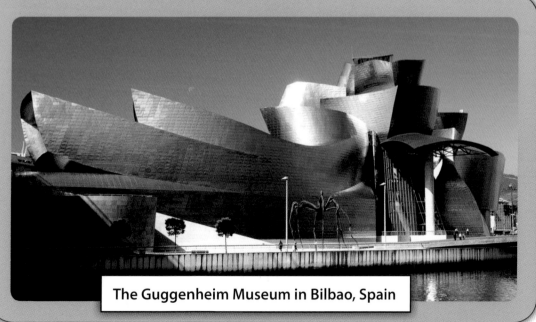

The Guggenheim Museum in Bilbao, Spain

Cube Constructions

Carla Barrios is an architect who designs buildings that are shaped like rectangular prisms. When she is designing, she likes to make models of her buildings by stacking 12 cubes on top of one another.

Solve It!

a. How many different model buildings could Ms. Barrios make? *Hint:* Each model must use 12 cubes.

b. Draw diagrams of the models she could make.

c. Explain how you know you have worked out all the different buildings Ms. Barrios could design.

Use the steps below to help you answer the problems.

Step 1: Use 12 small cubes and arrange them to form a rectangular prism.

Step 2: Draw the prism you have made.

Step 3: Rearrange the cubes to make another prism. Draw the prism.

Step 4: Continue rearranging the cubes and drawing the prisms.

Glossary

architects—people who design and plan new buildings and other structures

bases—special faces of solid figures, often the faces that they "sit on"; a prism is named by the shape of its bases

feature—a part or detail that stands out

foundation—the base on which something stands

geometry—the part of mathematics that studies lines, angles, and shapes

install—to put in

pentagon—a 2-D shape with 5 straight sides

plot—an area of ground

plumbing—the system of pipes and drains in a building or house

solid figures—geometric shapes with 3 dimensions: length, width, and height

stable—unable to be rocked or tilted

three-dimensional (3-D)—having 3 dimensions: length, width, and height

timber—wood that has been cut and made ready for building

trusses—a rigid framework of beams, bars, or rods

two-dimensional (2-D)—having 2 dimensions, length and width; plane figures are two-dimensional

vertex (plural: **vertices**)—a point or corner where 2 or more edges of a shape meet

wiring—a system of wires providing electricity

Index

Let's Explore Math

Page 5:
a. 6 faces
b. 12 edges
c. A cube

Page 8:
a. 8 vertices
b. Yes

Page 13:
Possible layouts include:

Page 18:
a. Triangle
b. 5 faces, 9 edges, and 6 vertices

Page 20:
a. Triangular prism
b. Hexagonal prism

Page 23:
a. It has two curved edges and two bases.
b. The bases are circles or ellipses.
c. Answers will vary. Sample answer: Unlike a prism, a cylinder has no vertices.

Page 26:
a. A sphere has no edges or vertices.
b. Answers will vary.

Pages 28–29:
Problem-Solving Activity
a. Ms. Barrios could make 10 different buildings.
b.

c. Answers will vary.